Nov. 2013

thE VAMPIRE UMPIRE

and OthEr StoRies foR ChildrEn

Published by Popsicle Books, 2013
an imprint of the Perera Hussein Publishing House

ISBN: 978-955-0041-05-3

Printed by Darshana Marketing Enterprises (Pvt) Ltd

 To offset the environmental pollution caused by
printing books, the Perera Hussein Publishing House
grows trees in Puttalam – Sri Lanka's semi-arid zone.

thE VAMPIRE UMPIRE

and OthEr StoRies foR ChildrEn

Edited by
Ameena Hussein

Popsicle Books
COLOMBO

For Aaliyah

Imagination encircles the world — Albert Einstein

CONTENTS

THE VAMPIRE UMPIRE
Afdhel Aziz

Frederico was a very unusual vampire bat. While all of his family liked sleeping upside down in trees and flying around at night, he preferred playing cricket.

His family had moved to Sri Lanka a long time ago from South America where they had originally lived. Frederico liked living in Sri Lanka — he liked having fish curry for breakfast, he liked going to the hill country with his family for their holidays…but the thing he liked most about Sri Lanka was that everyone played cricket.

Frederico loved cricket: he loved the sound the ball made as it snicked against the bat, the smell of fresh cut grass, the sight of fielders lunging for a catch....he even dreamed about it at night and knew everything there was to know about the rules of cricket.

But Frederico was a vampire bat, and had tiny hands which weren't very suited for bowling and batting, (it's true — bats really do have hands). So he found it particularly difficult to get anyone to let him play.

"Please, please, pick me, pick me," he would cry at school, while the rest of his friends chose teams. His friends, who all loved Frederico, hesitated.

Kannadi Polanga spoke up. He was a skinny lizard with a big pair of glasses, which he kept pushing up his nose as he spoke.

"Er...Frederico....how are you going to hold a bat?" he asked gently. "You've got hands but ....they can't really hold a bat." Frederico fluttered around in ever more agitated circles.

"I don't know...maybe you could tie it to my wings?" he cried.

Boo the bear was another of Frederico's friends, a big shambly bear with a shy grin. Boo said, "But Frederico how can you bowl a ball? It would be way too heavy for you."

"Um....maybe I could carry it in my mouth and throw it at the batsman?"

The situation looked bad. Finally Frederico piped up: "Why don't we take it to Mr Perera? Maybe he can help us with the answer."

Everybody brightened up. Mr Perera was a gecko who ran the local library and was generally considered to be the wisest gecko in the town. In addition, he was also in charge of the local Cricket Association. If anyone knew the answer, it would be him.

Mr Perera listened to their story very carefully, nodding his head and asking a few questions. Finally, he cleared his throat and said:

"My friends, I am glad that you have been able to come here today to share your story. I know you all have the best of intentions. You all love playing cricket. And you all love Frederico. And somehow we must find a way to bring Frederico into your game in a way that works for everyone."

Everyone nodded. Mr Perera had indeed summed it up well. He looked at them with his kindly eyes and said, "Well.....Frederico...don't you know all the rules of cricket? And can't you fly everywhere around the field very fast? Well then....why don't you be their umpire?"

Frederico was so excited that he looped the loop. "I would LOVE to be your umpire!" he said and everyone cheered. And he turned out to be the best umpire they had ever had. He didn't take sides, he was very very fair and everybody respected his opinion.

That night, when he went to bed, he smiled and thought to himself, "It just goes to show you that there's a place for everyone when you play... no matter what you look like or what you can do. I am Frederico and I am the world's first Vampire Umpire!"

THE SCARECROW

Asgar Hussein

After watching over the paddy field for a week, the Scarecrow began to get worried. The birds no longer seemed to be afraid of him. They came closer and closer, looking at him curiously. Some even flew over his head.

One day, he heard the crow telling the sparrows that he wasn't human.

"Look at that fellow! He thinks he can frighten us, but he can't even turn his head. He just shakes a little when a wind blows across the field."

The Scarecrow wanted to wave his arms and shoo them away. But he realized he couldn't move at all. He stood there feeling utterly helpless. A moment later, the crow landed on his shoulder.

"Look, my friends!" the crow cawed loudly. "See how I perch on him without any fear. He can't harm us at all."

The little sparrows circled the Scarecrow, chirping wildly. One landed on his hat and two others perched on his shoulders. Then they hopped all over his arms chirping, "He can't harm us. He can't harm us. He can't harm us in any way!"

The news soon spread that the Scarecrow was not dangerous. Many birds flew to him and settled on his hat and arms. There were babblers and orioles, an emerald dove, a shama and several parakeets that screeched loudly.

The Scarecrow was very upset and angry. The farmer had made him to scare off birds from the paddy field, but he was worthless now. There was nothing he could do. He felt miserable.

"What is my purpose if I can't keep the birds away?" the Scarecrow wondered. "Now my life is meaningless."

The birds noticed that he looked very sad. They felt sorry and tried to talk with him, but he didn't say anything. One morning, however, he couldn't bear it any longer and told a sparrow how he felt. "The farmer put me here for a reason – to scare you birds away and protect the paddy. He made me lovingly with wooden planks and old clothes stuffed with straw. For some time I kept you away, but now I am useless."

As he spoke, he looked sadly across the field. In the distance, he could see the farmer's village. "Don't worry," chirped the sparrow. "We birds are cheerful creatures. We will keep you company and entertain you with stories about our kind."

They told him delightful bird-tales. The shama sat on his shoulder and sang sweetly. He began to feel happy.

The sparrows told him tales about the shrewd crow. They said she could outwit humans, and even stole food from their kitchens. She had a habit of poking her black beak into pots and pans. She could also undo lunch parcels. She even flew over dinner tables to grab some tasty morsel of food.

Stories were also told about the majestic cock. He lived near the village, strutting proudly among the cackling hens. He was very tough and no polecat dared attack them. At sunrise, he crowed so loud to wake up the villagers that even the Scarecrow could hear him.

And then there was the emerald dove. She was a vain bird, and was always preening her feathers. She would fly to a nearby pond and gaze at her reflection. One of the sparrows liked to annoy her. So he would fly over the pond and drop a stone from his beak, sending ripples that cracked her image in the water.

From such tales, the Scarecrow learnt a lot about the birds. He also carefully watched those who flew around.

Then late one night, a strange-looking bird passed over him. He could see it clearly under the light of the full moon. It flew silently, and perched on the branch of a tree near the field. It had enormous eyes and a stout body. It looked so different from the other birds that he felt scared.

In the morning, when he told the sparrows what he had seen, they said, "Oh, that's the owl."

"The owl?" he asked. "It looked quite strange."

"Yes, it's a mysterious bird," they said. "It sleeps at daytime in some secret place. It goes hunting in the dark, looking for small creatures like rats to eat."

In this way the Scarecrow learnt more and more about life around him. He was quite happy. The paddy field was a charming place to be in. A gentle breeze often blew across, giving him a pleasant feeling. In the distance, he could see yellow butterflies flitting from flower to flower.

The birds saw him as a good friend. The sparrows chirped and cheeped on his arms. The shama sat on his hat and sang. The babblers, orioles and parakeets flew around him joyfully. The crow and emerald dove came to him for a chat. His life seemed to be meaningful.

But as the days passed, the Scarecrow began to feel miserable again. "How fortunate these birds are!" he told himself as he watched them play in the air. They had such freedom, while he was stuck to the field. How he wished his arms would turn to wings! How he wished he could fly high in the blue skies!

Now the Scarecrow saw no happiness in his own life. He wanted to fly away from the field and go far beyond. He wanted to see the world from up high as a bird would. He wanted to see the hills and plains, the rivers and waterfalls. He longed for the freedom of the skies.

One day, he saw a great bird soaring high. It had large elegant wings, and he gazed as it circled the sun. "What a magnificent bird!" he thought. "Such strength and grace!"

Suddenly, the bird plunged down. The sparrows cried, "The eagle! The eagle!" and fled in every direction.

The eagle swooped low where the chickens lived. It tried to snatch a hen with its talons. As the other hens clacked and clucked in terror, the cock rushed forward to save her. He attacked flapping his wings wildly, but the eagle was too strong. It struck out with its beak so fiercely the cock was thrown back. It then picked up the unfortunate hen in its talons and carried her off.

The sparrows and the other birds trembled in fear. Now that the eagle had come, they were no longer safe. They told the Scarecrow, "The eagle is a terrifying bird. It will take that poor hen to its nest high up among rocks. Then it will rip and tear her apart with its beak and feed her to its young."

The eagle came again the next day. As soon as they saw it soaring through the clouds, the birds scattered away. They flew as fast as they could and hid themselves. The Scarecrow knew why, for they had told him that the eagle had very sharp eyesight. Even from a great height it could spot a little bird in an open field.

The Scarecrow gazed as the eagle soared gracefully in the sky. "It is truly a magnificent bird," he thought. "And what fine wings it has! If only I could fly like that and see the world below."

Suddenly the eagle swooped down, and with its talons, caught a sparrow in mid-air.

It attacked so fast that the Scarecrow was shocked.

Later, when the other birds came out of hiding, he told them what had happened. The sparrows in particular were very sad. They huddled together on his arms and cried, "We will never see our friend again!"

The Scarecrow noticed how things changed after the eagle came. The birds were no longer cheerful. They now looked up at the sky with a frightened look. The shama hardly sang, and when he did there was a tone of sorrow in his voice.

However, the Scarecrow secretly admired the eagle. He was impressed by the grace of its flight. "What a magnificent bird it is!" he kept telling himself. He looked at the other birds and thought how weak and ordinary-looking they were compared to it.

Before long the eagle was back. This time it circled over the paddy field, casting its great shadow upon it. Then it landed right in front of the Scarecrow.

The great bird folded its wings and stared at him. He felt nervous and afraid seeing it so close. It had fiery eyes and a hooked beak. But he was also filled with admiration because it looked so powerful.

"What a sad life you live here," said the eagle. "You will stay stuck to this field until you waste away."

The Scarecrow somehow found the courage to reply. "Yes, that's true," he said, "But what can I do?"

"Well, I can help you," said the eagle. "With my powerful talons I can lift you away from this field. I can soar with you through the skies. We can travel far and wide. And from up high, you'll see great mountains and rolling plains. You'll see jungles and lakes. You'll see mighty rivers and waterfalls."

"How I wish to!" cried the Scarecrow. "Please carry me away and let me see the world!"

"That I will do," said the eagle. "But first, I must ask you a little favour."

When the Scarecrow said he would do anything, the great bird looked very pleased. It said, "Today I saw no birds around here. They must have fled as soon as they saw me in the sky. I want you to tell me their hiding-places."

The Scarecrow was silent for a while. He knew where the birds were hiding. They had told him what fine places they had found to escape from the eagle.

He felt sad to betray them, but the eagle's promise was too hard to resist. So he gave away their hiding-places.

The eagle spread its wings and soared into the air. Before leaving, it told the Scarecrow, "I'll be back once I finish with the birds. And then I'll fly high with you across the skies."

The eagle took the birds by surprise. One after the other, they were attacked in their hiding-places. There was no chance for escape.

Many were caught in the nearby woods. The eagle darted through it and snatched some parakeets and orioles. The sparrows and babblers were attacked as they hid among the bushes.

The emerald dove had taken shelter in the hollow of an old tree. She was sure she would be safe there, but the eagle thrust its beak in and took her out. The crow was caught in the shade of a plantain grove.

The shama was also attacked. As he came out of a bush to grab a worm, the eagle swooped down on him. He struggled as it carried him off in its talons, and a few feathers drifted down when they passed over the village.

Soon it was all over. The eagle returned to the field. It stood proudly before the Scarecrow and said, "Thanks to you, I and my young ones had a great feast. The birds were quite tasty!"

The Scarecrow did not feel too sad. After all, he now had a chance to fly high and see the world. He longed to see everything the eagle had described. He felt so excited!

He looked at the eagle hopefully and said, "I did as you asked and told you where the birds were hiding. Now you must keep your promise."

"Of course!" said the eagle. It then rose in the air and fixed its sharp talons on the Scarecrow's shoulders. As it pulled, the soil under him was loosened. A moment later, the great bird was able to lift him up.

Together they soared into the blue sky. As they rose higher and higher, the Scarecrow felt very excited. He could see the paddy field and the village become smaller and smaller. "I'm free at last!" he said.

Far and wide they went, the eagle carrying the Scarecrow in its talons. The world below was so enchanting. He gazed down at the woods and hills, the rivers and waterfalls. He was filled with wonder.

"It is all so beautiful," he told the eagle. "More beautiful than I ever imagined."

"Yes," said the great bird. "But now I'm going to take you to the finest place of all!" The eagle changed direction.

The Scarecrow was delighted. Even as the wind rushed against his face, he kept gazing at the scenery below. How wonderful and free he felt so high in the skies! He wanted this to last forever.

Soon they were over a mountainous area. Here the eagle began to descend. As they went lower, the Scarecrow saw a large nest built in rocks.

"That is my place," said the eagle. "And I want you to meet my young ones."

The Scarecrow was quite annoyed. He could hear the young ones screech as they got closer.

Suddenly the eagle released its talons and dropped the Scarecrow. He fell on a large rock near the nest. Then the great bird landed and came towards him. He felt a little frightened, for its eyes now seemed to be ablaze.

"How can you treat me like this?" asked the Scarecrow. "Did I not betray the birds so that you could have a great feast?"

"That is true," said the eagle. "But you are just a useless Scarecrow. In fact, I know only one thing you are good for."

The eagle attacked him fiercely. It ripped and tore him apart with its powerful beak. Then it used the straw in his body to make the nest more comfortable for its young ones.

Hunting Mangoes

Mary Anne Mohanraj

In the long, lazy afternoon, under the shade of a wide-leafed coconut palm, a brother and sister were quarreling. This was nothing new; Arun and Ziya had been born in the same moment, under the same star. Their exhausted mother would tell anyone who asked that they had been fighting ever since that day. Oh, they would unite quickly enough against a common enemy — Raju the Thief, for example, who had a habit of sneaking sweetmeats out of their tiffin tins. But in the absence of a common enemy, they made do fighting each other. Both twins liked nothing better than a good argument; and if a bit of hair-pulling or arm-twisting served as punctuation, all the better.

Today's disagreement was typical; they fought over which one was better. Not better at anything in particular, just better. Ziya was a sturdy, broad-shouldered girl, who at twelve years old was already taller than her father, and stronger than him too. She'd earned the nickname Elephant in their village, and wore it with pride. Ziya had inherited her great-grandmother's farming physique, and loved nothing more than lifting heavy objects and dropping them in Arun's way.

Arun, by contrast, was slender and small. He couldn't lift the things Ziya carried with ease, but he had his own methods for dealing with her. He was agile and quick, and often before she had time to put, say, a boulder in front of his bedroom door, he was up and over and out – taking a high window if need be, or even going over the roof. Everyone called him Monkey, and it suited him well.

"Strong is better!"

"Quick is better!"

"Strong!"

"Quick!"

"Strong!"

"Quick!"

Their arguments rarely offered much in the way of nuance, but they did have the advantage of great enthusiasm and volume.

"Elephant! Monkey! What is the matter with you? You are giving your poor mother a terrible headache."

Their mother, looking even more tired than usual, fixed them with her most threatening gaze.

"She started it!" Arun proclaimed.

Their mother frowned. "I don't care who started it, I want to know who will finish it!"

Ziya said, "But Amma, we can't agree. I think it is better to be strong —"

Arun interjected " — and I think it's better to be nimble and quick!"

Their mother sighed. "Well, I will tell you what, my creatures. I am hungry, and if you go over to the orchard and pick me a perfectly ripe mango from one of the trees, I will tell you the answer to your difficulty."

The twins quickly agreed, because the only thing they liked better than an argument was an adventure, and they had never been allowed to go all the way to the mango tree by themselves

before. Their mother turned and went back inside to find a nice book, and before six blind men could guess at the shape of an elephant, the pair of them were off.

They had no trouble running down the hill, through the jungle, to the riverbank. But when they reached the river, they discovered a dilemma.

"Do you think Amma knew the bridge had been washed away?" Arun asked, hesitating as he looked down at the tumbling muddy waters.

"No, of course not," Ziya said scornfully. "She knows that you're too weak to wade the river in full flood."

He bristled. "Oh, and you think you're so strong."

"I know I am," Ziya said calmly. And with that, she tied up her skirts and began wading her way across the river, not looking back at her brother stranded on the shore. Ziya planted her feet firmly, letting the water rush up against her, deeper and deeper, climbing up legs and belly and chest, until it was almost to her chin. Only then, at the deepest point, her toes digging into the silty bottom, did Ziya turn to look for her brother. Who, at that very moment, whipped past her, laughing, clinging to a swinging vine. "Wheeee!!!!"

Arun landed safely on the other side, in a stumbly tumble of limbs, and Ziya joined him a few moments later, wringing out her skirts as she came. "I would have carried you, you know. If you'd asked."

"I didn't need your help," Arun replied.

"Fair enough," Ziya said. And they went on. Up up the slope, across the rice paddy, through their father's grape arbors, until finally they reached the stand of mango trees. And there they found another problem.

"How are we supposed to get them down?" Ziya asked. The fruit hung just out of her reach, and there were only a few spindly branches to climb. If she tried, Ziya knew, the branches would crack beneath her weight.

"I can do it," Arun said. He ran back a few feet, turned, took a running leap, and made it into the branches. Then, like the Monkey he'd been named, he swarmed up the tree until he was safely tucked in among the ripe fruit. He pulled his knife out of his back pocket, picked the ripest, glowingest of the mangoes, and began to peel it.

Ziya didn't bother to remonstrate with her brother, to remind him that they were supposed to be bringing a mango back for their mother.

The scent of ripe mangoes was heady in the air, and she couldn't blame him for giving in to temptation. She would do the same, if she could only reach the succulent fruit. No way up. Not for her. But if she couldn't come up — well, the solution was simple, wasn't it? The mangoes had to come down.

She had just enough fellow-feeling for her sibling to pick a tree in which he wasn't ensconced. She stepped back a few feet, just as Arun had, took a few thundering steps forward, and SLAM — into the trunk went the meaty part of her shoulder. It hurt, but not as much as her stomach hurt, craving those mangoes. Ziya pulled back, and then slammed again. And again. And on the fourth slam, it happened. The trunk cracked, the top half came tumbling down, and a flood of mangoes rained down on her. Aaahhhh....

By the time they had both eaten their fill, the sun was coming down, and the last of the mangoes were gone. They were both too full and too tired to fight anymore; they had found a rare moment of peace. When Ziya and Arun felt like this, they rather liked each other, and sometimes, they could imagine a future when they were old and tired enough that they liked each other most of the time. Right now, they leaned against each other, in a messy, sticky nest of tree branches and peeled mango skins.

"Do you think this is what Amma intended all along?" Ziya asked lazily.

"I doubt it," Arun said. "She probably wanted us to learn some lesson about working together. I could have let you carry me across the river, after all."

"And I could have picked you up at the trees, so you could reach high and pick a mango for her."

"She would say that we're better together than we are separately." Arun frowned. "Do you think she'll be terribly disappointed, that we didn't learn the lesson she wanted?"

Ziya shook her head. "Don't be silly. We haven't bothered her in hours. Our mother will be thrilled."

"Oh, good," Arun said. "A happy ending after all."

"Yes," Ziya agreed. And as the sun slipped under the treetops, they closed their eyes, snuggled a little closer, and cheerfully fell asleep.

THE BLUE STONE

Pia Sonderegger

This is a secret. But if you tell anyone it will not matter, as nobody will believe you. I found a magic stone.

Now you will think, oh no, another one of those who believe in magic. Before you think that way, listen to this and then make up your mind.

I found it three months ago on my way to school. I usually walk to school with my best friend who lives on our street and my brother who is two years older than I and thinks he is smarter than everybody else. On that special day, I walked alone as my friend was sick and my brother was riding his new bicycle and refused to let me go with him as he wanted to show it off all by himself. That was going to be his big loss as his bicycle got stolen, but that is a different story.

As I walked along I kicked some pebbles by the side of the road as I usually do. You guessed right – the next thing I was going to kick made me stop at once: a big blue stone, and when I dusted it on my right sock it shone beautifully. I quickly put it in my pocket and looked around. There were several other school children about twenty meters behind me, but they were engrossed in conversation. I ran all the way to school and locked myself in the toilet. In the dim light I examined the stone. It reminded me of a fish I had caught once, deep blue and reflecting. It fit nicely into my fist.

As the school bell rang, I got out of the toilet and then the magic started. Our schoolteacher rushed past and patted me on the shoulder. Someone peeped out of a classroom door and smiled broadly. I turned around but there was no one, only me. The person smiling at me was the prettiest girl in school who had always treated me like air. The list goes on and on, from the presentation I gave in

class and which everyone applauded to lunch break when I found myself with more food offered to me than I could eat in a week, to end of school when about ten children wanted to walk me home. Call me a liar. Maybe there were nine children walking with me. Maybe no one liked his lunch packet that day. Maybe my presentation was funny. Maybe that girl is beautiful only to my eyes, and maybe our teacher was in a good mood. BUT. It had never happened before, never in my life.

In the afternoon I managed to go alone and hide the blue stone in a place I will not tell you. I went home, got scolded for being out without telling anyone, had to do all the sweeping and stacking of firewood and dinner turned out to be my least favorite meal to put it politely. In the night I could not sleep. I realized my good luck depended on the blue stone.

The next morning I did not have time to collect the stone before school. The whole day was such a disaster that all I want is forget it quickly. Never again am I going anywhere without my magic stone, I promised myself.

From then on the stone has always been in my pocket and luck on my side. I pass all exams with top marks. 'She' writes me love letters every other day. I found my brother's bicycle when he lost it and he takes me to school on it, me sitting on the handlebar and my best friend at the back. I became cricket captain of our team and the fastest swimmer in school.

You must think I am the happiest luckiest chap around. I say, the luckiest maybe, but my happy careless days are over. Imagine what will happen if I lose that stone! I worry about it every second, and it haunts my dreams in the night.

I wonder sometimes who owned the blue stone before and whether that person left it by the road on purpose. So, if you find it some day, it is unlikely that I simply lost it.

MINNIE THE SPY

Ameena Hussein

Minesha lay the table in a bad mood. She slammed the plates down, hurriedly arranged the cutlery alongside in a higgledy piggeldy manner and purposely kept the water glasses on the left side of the plate, instead of the right. A high screech came from the next room, "Quietly, child! Must you make a huge noise while working?" Minesha scowled to herself but managed to utter a penitent, "Sorry, madam." As she left the dining room to go into the kitchen Minesha wondered how on earth she had got into this situation.

Her mind wandered back to the day her mother read out the advertisement in the national newspaper.

WANTED: A SPY

The Ministry of Minors is looking for a smart young girl, aged twelve, to participate in an undercover operation to break a notorious child labour ring.

Mrs Pieris turned towards Minesha labouring at scales on the piano. "Minnie! You always say your life is boring and that you need some excitement. Here is, excitement handed to you on a platter." Minesha rose from the stool and stood behind her mother. There it was in black and white. A small square of text asking for applications to be sent within the week with a passport sized photograph. It was too perfect to believe.

Ever since Minesha was a little child, she had dreamt of being a spy. She fantasized about saving the country from alien invaders or cracking the mystery of blue potatoes. She poured over Famous Five stories and wished she had her own Gang of Five to pursue her adventures. Two weeks after reading the advertisement, Minnie was engaged in her favourite pastime once again. She lay down in the grass in her back garden and squinted through the leaves of the mango tree imagining scenarios where she was saving the world.

"Mineshaaa!" a voice sang over the short boundary wall that separated her from her best friend next door. Annoyed at her interrupted day dream of receiving the country's highest medal from the President herself, for solving the mystery of the monkey men, Minesha dusted herself off and galloped towards the wall. Straddling the partition with legs swinging back and forth sat the strangest figure. Dressed in black with an oversized sombrero hiding half his face and a red cape billowing behind him he motioned to Minesha to clamber behind him. "Come on up pardner, we gotta ride over yonder. There is a damsel in distress we need to save." Minesha hauled herself onto the wall and together they made a riding motion as if on a horse. Occasionally the caped stranger would swing an imaginary whip as if to urge his horse onward and faster. They both leant forward, imagining the wind whipping their hair and the landscape flying by. After a few minutes of this pantomime, Minesha said, "Listen Dileepan, I will be going away for a few months. My grandmother is ill and my mum thinks it's best I go and live with her for a while." The riding came to a sudden halt. The caped figure slowly removed his sombrero and turned to face Minesha. "But..." he began before he stopped. "Minnie, we can still chat on Facebook right?" Minesha frowned. "I'm not sure how internet connections are over there. She lives in a village Dileepan, she doesn't even have a computer. But don't worry I will take my cell phone with me and we can always text." Dileepan's face fell. "My phone has been confiscated," he mumbled. "It's so unfair! Everyone in class uses a phone but I am the only person Mrs Fernando picks on. She just hates me," he whinged. Dileepan was in the same school as Minesha but he was one year younger. "Oh! Mrs Fernando," she moaned. "I know how dreadful she can be. When she was my class teacher she made all of us write a thousand times: You will not be punished for your anger, you will be punished by your anger. Anyway," Minesha comforted him, "you will get your phone next week. She only takes it for the weekend right?" Dileepan nodded dolefully as he slipped down his side of the wall and trudged into his house. "I'll try to write," Minesha shouted. "I promise!"

Minesha couldn't believe that just a week before she was going through a flurry of interviews with serious looking men and women who sat across her from a table and studied her posture and asked her to walk up and down and do strange things like laying the table, sweeping and cleaning. At one point Minnie asked her mother if she was being interviewed to be a spy or for something else, which is when her mother, broke the news to her. "Darling," she said gently, as she led Minesha upstairs and sat her down in her room. "There are some nasty people who are taking children and making them work in houses for almost nothing. Now you know having children work for you is illegal. Children should go to school, they should play, they should enjoy life. But everyone is not as lucky as you are. Some children are sent off to work so that they can earn money for a bunch of mean and nasty people. Some of these children are even kidnapped. So the Ministry of Minors is trying to catch these horrible men and women and they need a smart young girl to help them do it."

The next day over a mug of hot chocolate milk Minesha listened to the nice young police woman who explained what she would have to do. "We will be with you every step of the way. Don't worry you will never be alone, but you cannot let on to the gang that you are not what you really are. You will have to be a master actor. Can you do it?" Minesha nodded her eyes shining. Here at last adventure was coming into her boring life. Here at last she was going to be a spy!

Three weeks later, Minesha dressed in a simple cotton dress and rubber slippers, her hair neatly braided in two plaits found herself at the front door step of a house in a neighbouring town. Holding the hand of a police woman who was dressed similarly and who gave her a reassuring wink, they waited for the door to be opened. At last they heard the shuffling of bare feet on the floor and a little girl no more than nine stood at the door. "Yes?" she inquired shortly in an unfriendly manner. The police woman began to speak, "Is the madam at home?" she inquired." I was told to come for a job and I have brought my daughter as well." Leaving them without a word, the little girl disappeared inside a back room. After a few minutes a pale faced woman with dark black hair came out with the little girl hiding behind her voluminous skirt. "Well?" she barked. After listening to the young woman's rehearsed speech, Minesha found herself being ushered into the kitchen while her supposed mother was shown around the house.

That night was the first of many uncomfortable nights Minesha was to have. The police woman and she were to share a small room the size of a shoe box. The toilet was outside on the far side of the unlit garden. She was to do light house work while the police woman was employed as cook and Woman Friday about the house. Minesha soon discovered the house was a zoo. It's more like a railway station the police woman told her later that night, as they shared notes and conversed in whispers. A steady stream of young women accompanied by little girls would come into the house and later be herded out to various places of employment. Mrs Moneybags, as Minesha nicknamed the pale faced woman, seemed to be in charge of the operation and she had a few male assistants as well. Mrs Moneybags was quite the dragon and Minesha soon learned to hop nimbly from one task to the next when she was around. In the meantime, the police woman, Nelum, was busy gathering her evidence. It was all going rather smoothly and Minesha soon learned from Nelum that before the week was out, the ring would be busted, when suddenly things started to go all wrong.

It began when Minesha was ordered to pack her bags and await her new place of employment. For the first time she saw Nelum look confused and then Minesha knew she was in big trouble. First, Nelum tried the crying Sri Lankan mother act. That didn't work. Then she tried the hysterical Sri Lankan mother act. That too didn't work. She finally tried the weeping, hysterical fainting Sri Lankan mother act. That did get her a few moments of reprieve but was still of no avail. With Nelum wailing on a side, Minnie thought quite believably, Minesha found herself being taken firmly by the hand towards the door and propelled outside into the bright sunshine. She was bundled into a small car with two strange people inside it. They gruffly asked her to crouch down at the back and not look out at all. They prodded and poked her until Minesha curled herself up very small into a ball. She could hear soft chatter between them. A man and woman were discussing what they were going to have for dinner. They didn't seem too worried about little Minesha at the back and after some time Minnie thought they had quite forgotten about her. She stretched her legs out and looked out through the window and upwards towards the sky. She saw many telephone wires and phone company towers, she saw birds and Buddhist flags and clocktowers and then she saw something quite strange. She saw a huge windmill but not just one she saw a number of windmills. Minesha gave a shiver of excitement, she knew just where she was. She was in Puttalam in the north west of the country. It was where her grandparents lived and where she had spent many holidays. Immediately, Minesha began plotting her escape.

They had been driving for over one hour with Minnie drifting in and out of sleep when the car stopped suddenly. It was dusk and light was fading fast. Minesha felt a bony hand grip her wrist and she was yanked out of the car. Her eyes blinking fast, she looked around and took stock of her situation. She was in a garden with flowering bouganvilleas and large mango trees. There was a dark old house looming in the shadows with a dimly lit verandah. Minnie was gently nudged towards the steps and as she began climbing them, she came face to face with the most evil faced man that she had ever seen. Minnie froze. She couldn't move forward, neither could she run away. It was as if her feet were stuck to the steps with Superglue. A finger prodded her onwards but Minnie seemed to be in a frozen state of panic. Mr Wicked whose name she discovered was Suresh reached out and dragged her up sending her flying into the house with a well aimed shove. "There you go," he said quite cheerfully.

That night, lying on a dirty mat in the kitchen with a bag of rice as a pillow, Minesha began to fret. She wondered if she would be ever found by Nelum and the rest of the police team and if she would ever see her parents again. A lone tear trickled down her cheek, but she wiped it briskly away and told herself she cannot cry, she was Minnie the Spy – she had to keep calm and plan how to escape this horrible situation. By the by she fell asleep and only woke up when the village cock began to crow at daybreak. She heard a creaking upstairs and knew Mr Wicked would be down soon. She hurriedly rushed about washing her face, brushing her teeth in the kitchen sink and plonking a kettle on the fire to make morning tea.

"Today," Mr Wicked began wheezily. "is a busy day for me and you, my girl. My grandson is coming to spend the day with some friends. We need to give them a lavish lunch and high tea. A woman will come from the village to do the cooking, you will have to clean the house, lay the table and assist the cook. Off you go now. Busy! Busy! Busy!" Minnie

didn't utter a word. She wouldn't have been able, if she wanted to. That entire morning, she was run off her feet and when a car with screaming boys arrived at lunch time, she didn't even have time to peep out and see who they were.

Lunch time arrived and with it the shock of her life. As Minesha walked out of the kitchen with a steaming platter of rice, she didn't know who was more surprised. Herself or Dileepan. She saw him open his mouth and form the word Minnie. Minesha knew she had to do something to stop him. So she did. She threw the platter of rice at the table, sending smithereens of porcelain and grains of rice just everywhere! All hell broke loose and Minnie ran for it. She could hear the man screaming in rage and anger, "I told them not to bring me a crazy coot and that is just what they did. I could have been killed in my sleep. She is a crazy girl, that one. She has a mad gleam in her eye. I could tell it from the minute I saw her!" Soon his voice got fainter and fainter as Minnie ran deep into the coconut plantation that surrounded the house. She saw a foot path leading towards a thicket of trees and she bounded towards it in double quick time. Pausing for breath Minnie wondered how she could get a message across to Dileepan that she was kept as a child servant in the house. All afternoon she sat by a small pond of water that was enclosed in the thicket. There was silence all around except for the occasional chatter of monkeys, the cry of a brahminy kite and the squawk of a jungle fowl. After a while of wandering and some exploring, Minesha found a large tree with a hollow trunk. Clambering inside she soon fell asleep.

Minnie woke up to a strange squelching noise. It was a familiar noise in an unfamiliar place and while she was trying to figure it out, she gasped as she caught sight of a caped intruder. "Dileepan!" she whispered. Dileepan froze. He looked around wondering where the voice was coming from. "Over here!" Minnie gesticulated frantically all the while hoping Dileepan had come alone. After she and Dileepan had settled down inside the hollow he told her what had happened when she ran away. "After you left the old man went ballistic and started saying you were a thief and went off to get his goons to look for you. The other boys went with him but I stayed back saying I was not feeling well. Quick! We must get out of here before they come back. I have a plan."

The next night safely back at home, Minnie and Dileepan drank hot chocolate milk together and sighed deeply at their close call. "So do you always travel with your cape?" she teased him. Dileepan frowned. "No! only when I know that a damsel is in need of rescuing." Minesha tickled him furiously, "I was not a damsel in distress. I was an important cog in the wheel. I was part of the whole mission. Take it back! Take it back!" "Mercy! Mercy!" Dileepan squealed as they tumbled together. "Ok! I take it back. I take it back." Minnie stopped her assault and they both laughed together.

Later that night when she was tucked into bed, Minnie told her mother how she and Dileepan had hidden in the hollow staying motionless and utterly silent while Mr Wicked and his boys searched all around. Luckily, earlier, Dileepan had the presence of mind to erase all their tracks and hide the opening to the hollow with a large ball of thorny scrub so that they remain hidden. The next morning, they clambered out and followed an old trail out of the thicket that led to the main road. To Minnie's delight they were not far from her grandparents home who were rather astonished to see two battered and scratched children trudging up their pathway virtually in the middle of nowhere. A quick call to her mother brought the Special Division to take them back home. Mr Wicked was netted but more importantly, the child labour gang was caught and broken. Minnie and Dileepan were heroes at the Ministry and went on to have many more adventures together.

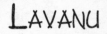

LAVANU

Alexandra Harris

With a slippery slap, the fish hit Ranuki in the middle of her forehead. It kept flapping around, gleaming silver under the fluorescent lights, gasping for water. The students all looked in astonishment at their teacher, Auntie Ursula – what had she just done?

Their chemistry teacher's antics were well known. She regularly berated her students. She drank coffee out of a beaker and kids avoided the first row of seats in the class because of her dreaded coffee and curry breath: She picked on all of the students, but she was especially cruel to Ranuki, the smallest girl in the class, whose experiments always seemed to go wrong.

"Why haven't you recalibrated that instrument?" she asked, while Ranuki shook in fear, her head down and her ponytail up. "And what are you doing staring at that silly fish again?"

Ranuki was looking at the poor trapped clownfish on Auntie Ursula's desk. The clownfish, whom the class called Minna, was swimming around in circles as usual in a small goldfish bowl. She had no pebbles, no friends, and most importantly, she had no sea anemone. The whole class had learned how important it was for clownfish to live with sea anemones. Ranuki's environmental science teacher, Mr Amit, had told them that they had a symbiotic relationship and depended on each other for survival.

"Clownfish and sea anemones are like salt and pepper. They belong together," she recalled him saying.

On this morning, Ranuki had been daydreaming again. She imagined herself riding on a beautiful blue dolphin, up through the darker waters of Lavanu to the surface, jumping in and out of the waves along the surface of the water with colourful fish as her companions.

Ranuki and her classmates attend the School of the Seas. They live in Lavanu, a land that is seventy-five percent underwater, so Ranuki often dreams of leaving the dark water behind and reaching the sun and sky many miles above her classroom. In her dreams, she sees Minna swimming free in the ocean. Unfortunately, on this particular day, Auntie Ursula saw that she wasn't doing her chemistry experiment and hadn't even turned on her Bunsen burner.

"Lazy girl!" Ursula screamed, and the whole class watched in shock as she reached into the small bowl on her desk, picked out poor wriggling Minna, and threw the fish directly at Ranuki. This was too much for the class. The other students stood up and rebelled.

"How can you treat her like that?" asked Niruja, the most outspoken in the class.

"Save Minna!" said Christopher. Niruja ran next door to find Mr Amit, the science teacher. He was sitting at his desk grading some papers.

Auntie Ursula has done something terrible!"

Amit, who was younger than old Auntie Ursula, was reluctant to get involved, but he followed Niruja anyway. What he found completely surprised him. A girl — his student, Ranuki — with a red mark on her face sat in one corner crying, and a boy stood in the middle of the room holding a flapping fish, saying "What shall I do?" All of the students were on their feet, talking over each other.

"What is going on here?" he asked Auntie Ursula. Instead of answering, she just looked at him defiantly, taking a swig of her coffee.

Mr. Amit, calmly taking the desperate fish from Christopher said, "Bring that fishbowl over here, please." Christopher ran to the front of the room to take the bowl from Auntie Ursula's desk.

"Give me that!" shouted Auntie Ursula, lunging at him, but she was too heavy and lost her balance while he deftly jumped out of the way. She collapsed on the floor and the children stepped over her, rushing around the room. Christopher grabbed the bowl and Mr Amit quickly put Minna in, rescuing her.

"I've had enough of these beasts," Auntie Ursula huffed, pulling herself up and hustling out the door.

"Just a moment," Mr Amit said, but she was already gone, coffee beaker in hand.

He turned to Ranuki, who had stopped crying.

"Are you all right?" he asked quietly.

"Yes," she said, peering out the large round window into the deep ocean.

"Come, I want to show you something. Follow me," he said, heading out the door of the classroom.

"What about Auntie Ursula?" asked Ranuki.

"I'm afraid she disrespected you and the fish. But I don't think you will be seeing her again," said their teacher.

"All of you, please come with me," he said, addressing the class.

The students looked at each other, shrugged and followed him out. Their teacher led them down the hall to the Descend/Ascend station.

The class crowded around the round station with its metallic gleaming surfaces. Mr Amit pushed a small button and the doors opened with a whooshing sound.

"Go on, everybody, get in, " he said. Nobody else was leaving the school at this time so the large pod was empty. Everyone piled in, crowding around the window at the back. No matter how many times they had travelled by desa pod, they were still fascinated by the view outside.

"Going up, level 3. Coral station," said Amit.

"Going up. Coral station," echoed a tinny female voice from the pod speaker. "Pass, please." Amit scanned his ID by the door.

"Accepted," said the robotic voice.

Silently they found themselves being pulled up from darker waters full of caves, seaweed and silvery fish, to sunnier, more colourful coral forests. Ranuki could barely contain her excitement.

"Minna, we're going up," she whispered to the fish, which she was now carrying. Minna seemed listless and dazed.

As they travelled up through the ocean, the teacher leaned in.

"Shall I tell you a bit about how we came to live underwater in Lavanu?" he asked.

"The Department of Underwater Living says it's because of global warming," said Christopher.

"All the ice melted and the water rose," said Niruja in her serious voice.

"Yes. But it all happened much faster than we expected," said Mr Amit. "When I was a boy, Lavanu was an island off Sri Lanka."

The students all gathered in a circle around Mr Amit.

"Tell us more," said Ranuki.

"We knew this day would come of course," said Mr Amit. He remembered when the Department of Underwater Living first broke ground, or dropped anchor, whatever the appropriate metaphor was. "Now you all carry your masks and BCDs along with your backpacks, and you can find them at any WaterMart, but it wasn't always so," he said.

"Did you used to be able to breathe outside without a mask?" asked Christopher.

"Yes, we did. I used to ride my bicycle outside on roads instead of swimming through the McDonalds!" The children gasped.

"Didn't you use trains?"

"Yes, instead of pods taking us to different buildings we had train stations to go from one city to the next."

"But isn't it better now?" asked Niruja. "The tourists like to come here. Especially the Germans and Australians. They say it's way more fun than the Maldives."

"They have hotels on stilts – pah! We have manta rays as pets," said Christopher.

"I have a new one at home. It's a purple-spotted one. All the celebrities have them now. They are the labradoodles of Lavanu," said Niruja proudly. She had clearly been reading too many of her mother's magazines.

"Yes, yes, but kids, we are getting off track," said Mr Amit.

"It is not better or worse, but it's very different. Yes, the tourists flock to Lavanu because right now it's a novelty, but it won't be for long. Soon all of the Maldivian hotels will need decompression chambers."

The students looked surprised.

"So the whole world will become like Lavanu?"

"I hope not," their teacher said.

With a dinging sound, the door opened and they found themselves on an underwater platform, in a bubble, with glass on all sides. It was a bit like sitting in an enormous greenhouse.

"Have you been here before?" asked Mr Amit. "No," said Niruja. "I thought it was off limits."

"Not always," said Mr Amit, laughing. "As an environmentalist, I have an access pass."

"Do you know what this place is?"

The children shook their heads, looking around in amazement at the beautiful colours, which they never saw at home or in school. Purple and red brain corals, wavy tendrils of orange, and the fish! All different colours of rainbow fish and parrotfish weaved in and out of the coral.

"This is the Coral Reef Rehabilitation Project," said Mr. Amit. "Our coral is being ruined by humans and by acidification. "

"Look, that cute little striped fish looks like Minna!" said Christopher. "Is it called a tiger fish?"

"No, silly. That's a clownfish," said Ranuki. Christopher never seemed to listen in class.

"Yes, that's right. That's a clownfish like Minna," said their teacher. "Many clownfish are in danger," he said.

"Why?" they all asked at once.

"Because of climate change, the ocean has become more acidic. You know what acid is, right? Like a lemon is acidic and sour. The acid affects clownfishes' sense of smell, so they can't find sea anemones. The anemone is that purple waving plant there, see."

"What happens when they can't find anemones?" asked Ranuki.

"They need those anemones for protection from bigger fish and other predators. If they can't find them they are vulnerable, and will be eaten. If global warming gets worse, some kinds of animals will become extinct. That means they will disappear completely."

The students looked sad and troubled.

"These are okay because they are protected in this refuge. We're going to leave Minna here, where she is safe," he said.

He pointed to the vacuum window valve, a round opening. "Ranuki, are you ready to let Minna go?"

Ranuki nodded silently.

"On the count of three, take her out and I will open the valve and you must quickly release her," he said.

"Goodbye, Minna," said the class.

"Have fun, Minna. I'll miss you," said Ranuki, fishing her out of the bowl and quickly releasing her through the vacuum valve, which expelled her gently into the ocean. Minna seemed overwhelmed, but soon made her way over to a purple anemone, gleefully swimming around with other clownfish.

"Look, our fish has found some friends! She seems happy now," said Niruja.

"But what about global warming? What can we do to help stop her from losing her sense of smell?" asked Ranuki.

"To stop climate change you should recycle and reuse, and use solar energy whenever possible. Turn off your computer and your lights when you're not using them to save energy."

"We have to protect our resources and respect the Earth. We cannot treat fish or manta rays simply as pets or things to use and throw away. We shouldn't be wasteful. We must respect the oceans and our environment." For once the room was hushed as the students contemplated what their teacher had just said, still watching the colourful fish and waving coral.

"Should I let my manta go free?" asked Niruja.

"That's a start," said Mr Amit, laughing.

"But not enough," added Ranuki. "Let's all make a pact to use less energy and not be wasteful. We can be a new club – the Protectors!"

"Or we could be the Friends of the Clownfish," said Christopher, excited.

They quickly put their heads together and began talking about what they could do next, while Mr. Amit agreed to be their faculty head. They all decided to make Ranuki their club leader. Ranuki's reputation changed forever from "the one hit by the fish," to "the one who protects the fish."

THE CUNNING CHENA CULTIVATOR VS. THE FOREST SPIRIT

Nanda P. Wanasundera

Haramanis, the villager of our story, is a chena cultivator. Very early each morning he would set off to the plot of jungle land he had leased from the government for the year, carrying a packet of rice and curry wrapped in banana leaf, which his wife cooked for him. He would first cut down the small trees, bushes and undergrowth and set fire to it. In a couple of days he would sow seed of different kinds like kurakkan, meneri and thala. He would dig a part of the ash-filled half acre, to soften the earth and grow vegetables. These vegetables — ladies fingers, brinjal, chillies, gourds and pumpkin — grew lush since the soil was fertile. Maize, yams and manioc were also grown. His harvest was bountiful but he could grow these for only two seasons. After that, his plot of land lost its fertility and he was too poor to artificially fertilize it. He would then, like all chena cultivators, move on to a new patch of forest to slash and burn and grow his crop once again.

The first time Haramanis entered his leased out plot of jungle he had a most uncomfortable feeling. He sensed that someone was watching him. Animal? Human? So he called out loudly: "Who is there?"

He got no answer.

He looked around and then cautiously walked around. There was not a deer or hare to be seen.

He experienced this strange feeling the next day as well, and the next. That evening, he told his wife about it. Feeling very concerned, she said she would leave their children with her mother and accompany him the next day. That fourth day they worked hard and long together and he felt no presence. Now, his plot was ready for cultivation.

On the fifth day with no thought except that of scattering the grain he carried in separate bags in a reed basket, he went to the land. There was no wind but suddenly he heard rustling from one spot in the jungle. Being sure it was an elephant, he stealthily made his way to a large tree on the opposite side, ready to climb it if an elephant appeared.

Suddenly, out of the blue, a voice was heard. It was not human, but not inhuman either. It was just different. It was heard distinctly but sounded like air from a tube hissing out. Haramanis, scolded himself for being scared in broad daylight but he found his hair standing on end.

"Don't be afraid. I am not an animal. I am not a human being either," said the voice.

Haramanis looked around. No human nor non-human being was to be seen. But he had heard the voice; that was for sure. Bravely he said, pretending anger: "Then what the devil are you?" His annoyance had got the better of his fear, and he almost chuckled that he had hit the nail on the head for villagers believed that devils lived in the jungle and were to be avoided.

"I am the spirit who lives in this place. This land is my domain."

"I do hope you are not an evil devil," said Haramanis. "I am wearing a suré — see this amulet with charmed oil in it; so neither you nor any spirit can harm me."

"I will not harm you. I am not a devil. I am a good spirit. I want to be your friend. I will protect you from evil spirits and even elephants and bears and leopards."

"That's mighty kind of you!" retorted Haramanis, who was getting tired of this conversation. After all, why waste time speaking with a being that he could not even see. He had plenty to do to sow his seed before the day was done. He added: "And why this kindness and offered protection? My gun is my protection against animals and this suré I wear against such as you."

"Guns don't fire sometimes; and surés can be powerless in the presence of really bad spirits. But I am not evil. I like you and want to strike a bargain."

"What is it?" queried Haramanis. Things are getting more and more curious, he thought to himself.

"For the protection I give you, you must give me something in return."

"What's that?" asked Haramanis. "So nothing is for free from even the devil!"

"Please don't call me a devil. I am a spirit and owner of this plot of land. I have supernatural powers. That's how I will protect you."

"So you are the government now! This land is owned by the government. You are the police too, I suppose, protecting me!"

"No, I am only a spirit but this land is where I live and other spirits treat it as my land. I don't encroach on their lands, and they don't on mine. Take my protection and give me half your harvest. That is all."

"So you eat food too? Bah! All these lies!" said Haramanis in disgust.

"Don't be rude to me. I can destroy your crops by bringing a pestilence on them. I can drive an elephant mad and have him destroy your plants. So the best thing for you to do is agree to share your harvest with me."

Haramanis was torn between being indulgent to the spirit or chasing him away with his own mantras or chants he had learned from his father and grandfather which were supposed to be potent against evil spirits.

He also felt he owed nothing to this interfering spirit – nothing. The government had leased this half acre of land to him; he had paid for it and now all he had to do was work very hard to scatter seed, keep the land safe from invading rodents, monkeys and marauding elephants and wildboar, and then gather the harvest. He was even willing to spend nights here bitten by mosquitoes to guard the land. So why labour to share his harvest?

But, realizing that it was wiser to cooperate, even though the request was absurd, Haramanis agreed to share the produce of the land. "You take all that is under the ground this season. The next season I take all that is under ground, you can have all the vegetables, grain and fruits that grow above ground." He had already hatched a plot to cheat this spirit.

"Agreed!" shrilled the spirit. "I won't be able to eat the stuff but I can enjoy it."

They did not shake hands on their agreement, nor sign a memorandum of understanding, but a bargain had been struck.

Utterly curious, Haramanis asked the spirit what he would do with the half harvest.

"Must I tell you my secret?"

"Yes, because we are friends now and partners in agriculture, too," said Haramanis. "There are no secrets between friends."

Sounding coy, the spirit said that he was very fond of Ran Menika, the young wife of the farmer in the house closest to the forest. "I will take the produce I get from this land and lay it at her doorstep. Then she can have better meals and look prettier and be healthy too."

Bah! Phew! Utter Nonsense! said Haramanis to himself, sending a stream of betel chewed saliva shot out like an arrow. This is a spirit and a half! In love with a human being! What is the world coming to? He wanted to, but did not ask the spirit why he was not offering his love to a female spirit. Maybe all spirits are unisex, he muttered under his breath. In any case it's none of my business; my business is to sow these seeds and get home before the sun sets.

The next day, was the day for planting cuttings of yams such as sweet potato, manioc and other tubers. This is how Haramanis normally did it: He planted a piece of stem of the required plant with a couple of leaves intact and in a couple of days it took root. But, this time he did not plant any cuttings. He pretended to be doing so but he had sown only all grain and vegetables and not one plant that would bear its produce under the ground. He did not feel guilty about not growing stuff to give the produce to the spirit because, according to the cultivator, there were done things and things not done; sensible things and utter nonsense. Sharing a harvest with a spirit was nonsense. He takes the trouble of preparing the ground, of planting and protecting the growing plants from wild animals, and here comes this nonsensical spirit asking for a half share just because he lived in the trees in this plot of land. He even had the audacity to say the land was his! And the produce demanded was to be laid at the doorstep of his lady love. That was a luxury a bodyless, and for that matter, mindless spirit could not aspire to. And who was to sweat and struggle to get the produce? He, Haramanis, the chena cultivator!

Chena cultivators usually build themselves a little watch hut wedged between a branch of the largest tree and its trunk, or on two adjacent branches. They stay in it all night, resting but ready to clang a metal bell they keep close at hand at the first sign of an animal invading their plot of cultivated land. Wild boar snorting around and elephants are the worst chena thieves. Hopefully, the cultivator is safe in his perch on the tree since he has selected a very strong and sturdy tree that not even the strongest elephant can shake or dislodge. Cheetahs and leopards climb trees, but luckily, being carnivorous, they do not prowl around in chenas.

Haramanis was not too comfortable sleeping nights out in the hut because of the companion on his land. But the spirit told him that he was never there at night. He roamed around and mostly stayed near Ran Menika's house to protect her and drive away other hovering spirits and animals from her home.

When the time for reaping the harvest was near, instinctively, Haramanis felt the presence of the spirit. When finally the harvest was gathered — all grain and vegetables — there erupted atmospheric havoc. The spirit indulged in a temper tantrum of hurricane velocity and sound. Haramanis heard loud thuds on the ground, violent shaking of tree branches with no wind, and even splintering of twigs and breaking of branches. These were flung on the ground. Lots of divul fruits came raining down from the trees on the edge of the chena. But Haramanis went on working though his heart was thumping. The spirit then resorted to his most powerful battle tactic. A terribly foul smell enveloped Haramanis. He tied the large handkerchief that was around his head over mouth and nose. He was near choking, but he went on working, pretending to be calm. Haramanis knew it was the spirit expressing anger that he got nothing from the harvest.

"What's all this?" shouted Haramanis, pretending to be very angry, while actually being scared. "For whose benefit are you putting on this show – breaking branches, raining divul fruits and even sending out a horrible smell?"

"I got no share. There was nothing for me."

"What can I do if the yams did not swell out and grow. A more powerful spirit must have cast the evil eye on this plot of land. Even my harvest of grain and vegetables is miserable. Next time you will be the lucky one. All the grain will be yours, and the pumpkins and fruit. I will have only yams and if things go like this time, I won't have anything. Then Ran Menika will grow fat and lovely because you will have so much to give her, and my wife and children will grow thin and pale with hunger." At the mention of Ran Menika the spirit subsided and peace reigned in the chena.

After selling his excess grain and storing the rest in bins and then having a few days of rest and recuperation not only from labour but from contact with the spirit, Haramanis was ready once again, for the next chena cultivation. They had celebrated the Sinhala New Year, it being April, and he had enough money to buy clothes for his wife and children, his parents and hers. He even had money to buy his wife a pair of gold bangles. It had been a good harvest. A tinge of regret overcame Haramanis. Was it the spirit's benevolence that had given him such a bumper crop?

This second season, the work to be done in the chena was less. The slash and burn part was not repeated.

He got his planting material ready. His wife noticed he did not have any seed or grain in the gunnysacks he was taking to the chena. He told her the Mudalali had hinted that yams would be fetching a good price in six months time. So he planted his yam cuttings all over his chena.

The spirit would once in a while converse with him, mainly to inquire when the harvest would be in. He was getting fonder and more protective of Ran Menika and dreaming of the day he would leave on her doorstep many bags of grain and vegetables. Haramanis would say there was plenty more time for the harvest. Grass was growing on the plot of land, as inevitably it would, and this appeared to the spirit as crops grown by the farmer.

Haramanis was getting cold feet as harvest-time approached. As it got close, he hardly slept in the tree hut. When his wife inquired he said his bones were older and less able to stand the cold out there. He was lucky, no animals invaded his land, and even if they did, no damage was done to what he had planted, because the produce was all underground.

Then, the yams he had planted were ready for pulling out. He told his wife that he would be uprooting the stuff the next night, which was a poya or full moon night, and he would do it in one go.

"Whatever for?" inquired his wife. "You normally take three or four days to uproot yams you grow and that's in only a part of the land. And, for goodness sake, why at night?"

"The astrologer told me to do it this way," lied Haramanis. "You, your two brothers and mine will help. That way we can get all the yams collected in one night. You know I want to make the most money possible since we are being offered land in that colonisation scheme and I am tired of chena cultivation. I shall move to proper cultivation in a government scheme."

So the yams were collected in one night by moonlight. And where was the spirit? Guarding Ran Menika's house and being happy just hovering around her compound and, this time Haramanis escaped the spirit temper tantrums.

Haramanis had no guilty feelings that he had cheated the spirit. However, he avoided his chena like the plague. In any case he did not have to return to it since chenas are cultivated only twice in the same plot of land.

But, he did hear, on the nights immediately following harvest time, the jungle trees close to his home being thrashed around with no wind. Loud muttering and scolding came to his ear, but mercifully they were directed only at him. He stayed indoors, certain that spirits do not come into villages and never into homes.

Things quietened down. Haramanis gave up chena cultivation and went to live in a colonisation scheme close by. With the forest being cleared by men using tractors and so many cultivators around, Haramanis believed the spirit had vanished. But he always wondered if Ran Menika found forest fruits and hives full of bees honey at her doorstep.

THE BLINK FAIRY

Sanjaya Senanayake

Have you ever wondered if fairies exist? The idea seems preposterous. I myself never used to believe in fairies – dismissed them as an absurdity – until I heard Saesha's story.

Although this story is about Saesha, a ten-year-old girl who lives in Colombo Heaven, the poshest suburb of the capital, it actually begins with a drink. Its creator and place of origin was a mystery; but it was so popular it became an international sensation. Because of some strange side effects, officials decreed that it was only for adults and not suitable for children. Apart from the taste it looked good too: the top half was fluorescent pink as if from the brightest of lava lamps, whilst its bottom half was the deepest blue, just like the colour of a tropical ocean. And what do you name a drink that's blue and pink? 'Blink', of course. Within a year, Blink was being consumed (known as "blinking") by adults everywhere around the world. Soon, "Blink parties" were the "in thing"; and, Colombo Heaven, got hooked. This might sound okay but, while Blink was a vision of beauty that tasted equally good, too much of it made adults behave oddly. They became irresponsible and silly and even the authorities were blinking. Yes, Blink appeared to be there for the foreseeable future.

Saesha's mother and father were delightful people – until they drank Blink, which they only did at Blink parties. She was usually the only child there, condemned to watch TV by herself while the adults' party raged on in an adjacent room. If you asked Saesha what Blink did to adults, she would tell you that at first they all became very loud and would laugh like hyenas for no apparent reason before eventually collapsing in a heap on the floor. Uncle Asoka, a fat man with a big moustache, had once taken so much Blink that he fell flat asleep in front of Saesha and began snoring. She made the best of the odd situation and used his chubby body as a comfortable footrest while she watched TV. What else was she to do?

At a particularly boring party, Saesha was sitting in the TV room talking to herself, as she sometimes did, when she heard a loud cough. She turned to see Aunty Rosie at the doorway. All the grown-ups at these parties were odd, but Aunty Rosie was one of the oddest. She was much older than Saesha's parents and wore the strangest combination of clothes, like a tight leopardskin outfit and a hat filled with bright feathers. To Saesha it seemed that Aunty Rosie had been to the zoo and brought back some of the animals. But this particular night, it was Aunty Rosie who was doing all the staring. Saesha, being a polite girl, asked her if anything was wrong.

"Wrong?" asked Aunty Rosie. "I've been standing here watching you for the past few minutes and you've been talking to yourself!"

"I do that sometimes," Saesha replied.

"Well, I don't like it. Only crazy people talk to themselves!"

Naturally Saesha was upset. She didn't like being called crazy especially by someone as crazy as Auntie Rosie.

"Got nothing to say for yourself? demanded Aunty Rosie.

Thankfully, her father appeared, just then.

"Rosie, what's the problem?" asked Saesha's father. He seemed vague and slow, which always happened to him after drinking Blink.

"Your daughter was having a chat. She was waving her hands around like crazy — but there was nobody in the room! Is she mental?"

Saesha turned to her father who to her surprise said, "Rosie, you know kids today: they're nuts!" And then to Saesha, "Come on, Saesha, stop jabbering to yourself! You're letting the side down." He left the room with Aunty Rosie who wore a smirk on her face.

Saesha was not a cryer, however, that night, she bawled her little eyes out as she contemplated this betrayal by her father. The next morning as she struggled out of bed and sadly meandered towards the kitchen, she was whisked up by a strong pair of arms that gave her a fierce embrace. It was her father.

"My little girl! How are you?"

It was as if last night had never happened. Saesha's father was his old happy self. He hugged her, kissed her and twirled her around in circles till she felt dizzy. They both collapsed on the floor in fits of laughter. Her mother walked in and smiled fondly. But even this couldn't erase Saesha's sadness. So she asked, "Thaththa, why didn't you help me against Aunty Rosie?"

"What are you talking about?" he asked a puzzled look on his face. "Did something happen?"

"Umm no, not really," she replied, "It's nothing." Saesha suddenly realised something else. Blink made you forget things. Her father was clueless about what had happened.

It was obvious to her that Blink was ruining her parents and she had to do something. She wasn't an especially religious child but she had been taught at school to respect all religions. That night in her bedroom, she prayed: "Lord Buddha, Jesus, Vishnu, God of Islam, God of the Jews, Barack Obama and Harry Potter, please help me. I have a great Ammi and Thaththi. They are wonderful except when they drink Blink. When blinking, they become different people, and not in a nice way. I'm afraid that one day they'll never return to normal. You are my last hope."

Saesha put a lot of effort into her prayer, and expected an immediate response. Unfortunately, praying is an uncertain business and no reply is guaranteed. She waited for weeks for a miracle which didn't come. After the initial disappointment, she forgot about the prayer and carried on with her life.

Two months later, Saesha awoke at night to find someone in her room. Astonishingly, even though she saw a figure silhouetted against the moonlight sitting at her desk, she was not afraid. She immediately turned on her bedside lamp and found herself in the presence of a most odd-looking creature. It had long black hair, large pointed ears, caramel-coloured skin, and two wings on its back. It was wearing blue jeans and a white t-shirt. In its right hand was a long stick with a star at its end.

"Hello," said Saesha.

The figure turned around to reveal the face of a beautiful girl.

"Oh, you're awake – good," said the stranger.

"Who are you?" demanded Saesha.

"I'm Reshmi. You asked for my help."

"I did?" asked a baffled Saesha.

"Yes, the prayer to help with your parents?"

"Oh, yes!" Then something occurred to Saesha. "Are you some sort of god?"

Reshmi laughed. "No. I'm the Blink Fairy."

"The Blink Fairy?" asked Reshmi. "What's that?"

"You know how the Tooth Fairy deals with teeth?"

Reshmi nodded.

"Well, the Blink Fairy deals with Blink-related problems."

"Oh my!" exclaimed Saesha. "Are there fairies for every drink? Like an Apple Juice Fairy?"

Reshmi shook her head. "Nope. But then again, Blink's not a normal drink. You see, it wasn't made by humans."

"Then by whom?" asked Saesha.

"Leprechauns," replied Reshmi. "In fact, Blink really stands for, 'Blue Leprechauns' Independence from the Nine Kingdoms'.

"Leprechauns? You mean the ones who leave a pot of gold at the end of a rainbow?"

Reshmi nodded. "Those are the ones. Most leprechauns are charming. But the Blue ones have a real chip on their shoulder. Think they are better than the rest of us in the Nine Kingdoms — the fairies, pixies, nymphs, imps, goblins, elves and gnomes — and they want their own country."

"But what's that got to do with Blink?" asked Saesha.

"After the Council refused their request for independence, the leprechauns got angry and planned their revenge. They brewed a magical drink, using rainbow colours, and flooded the human world with it. It's never happened before in our history."

"And that drink was Blink," said Saesha, finally understanding. "But why are they angry with humans? It's got nothing to do with us."

"They're not angry with you. It's because the leprechauns knew that the rest of us magical beings would have to fix all of your problems! I've been travelling all around the world non-stop for nine months trying to repair all the damage Blink has caused. Adults going crazy, wearing clothes in the shower, forgetting how to drive, burping uncontrollably, turning up to work in their pyjamas...the list goes on. Sound familiar?"

"Definitely!"

"Anyway, let's get down to business," said Reshmi, as an electronic tablet appeared in her hands out of nowhere. She flapped her wings and flew over to a startled Saesha.

Reshmi started reading from the tablet. "Lord Buddha, Jesus........have a great Ammi and Thaththi... love me a lot......wonderful...except when they drink Blink......my last hope."

"That's my prayer!" exclaimed Saesha.

"I know. Anyway, sounds like your parents' blinking is really worrying you?"

Saesha's shoulders slumped. "Blink is destroying them. I'm so afraid."

Reshmi put an arm around her shoulder. "You're not alone. I've spent months fixing families just like yours."

"Do you fix them all?"

"Most, but not all," Reshmi admitted.

Saesha gulped on hearing this. "Can't you use your magic to force them to stop blinking?"

Reshmi shook her head. "No. Fairy magic can't do that. All I can do is show them what's going to happen if they keep blinking. But the decision to change has to come from their hearts. Some parents change....but some do not."

Saesha gulped. "So, what do you do? Wave your magic wand and cast a spell?"

Reshmi laughed. "Gosh, no! This wand is only for sending text messages. What I'll do is sprinkle them with some fairy dust while they're asleep and let some dream magic do the rest."

Saesha shot up on hearing this. "Fairy dust? Can I see?

"I'm sorry. We only produce fairy dust when we fart."

"Really?"

Reshmi nodded. "Before a job, I always eat baked beans – great for fairy dust."

Saesha was astonished. "It's quite different from what you see in the movies."

Reshmi frowned. "Yes, Disney's got a lot to answer for."

"So do you like being the Blink Fairy?"

Reshmi shrugged. "It's not bad. But I'd rather be the Tooth Fairy."

"Why?" asked Saesha.

"Because the Tooth Fairy is filthy rich."

Reshmi started flicking the screen of the electronic tablet. "Okay, I've got an all-day job tomorrow in Peru. But I can book your parents for Tuesday night. How does that sound?"

"I think it should be fine."

"Brilliant. But there are some ground rules. At night, you might wake up to hear noises from your parents' room. Whatever happens, don't go in there, or you'll ruin everything. Do you understand me?"

Saesha gulped at this. "I understand."

"Good," said Reshmi. "Then in the morning, I want you to do something." Reshmi gave Saesha further directions. Then she vanished into thin air, leaving Saesha wondering whether she had just met a fairy or whether she was losing her mind.

However, as Reshmi had said, Saesha woke in the early hours of Wednesday morning to voices coming from her parents' room. It was clear that something unpleasant was going on.

"Please leave me alone!" cried out her mother.

"I didn't mean it! Please forgive me!" shouted her father.

Saesha wanted to help her parents but she remembered Reshmi's commands. So she remained in bed and covered herself with her blankets and pillows to muffle the noise. In the morning she followed Reshmi's instructions. She shot out of bed and climbed downstairs to open a cupboard that she'd never opened before. In it, she found many luminescent bottles of Blink. She took one and climbed the stairs. Her parents' bedroom door was ajar. She entered the room and saw her parents sitting in bed, clinging to each other, looks of terror on their faces.

"It must have been a dream," her father said.

Saesha's mother nodded. "Yes. But the same dream for both of us?"

Saesha's bemused father shrugged his shoulders. "I don't know. It just doesn't make sense."

Saesha walked right up to her parents and held up the bottle of Blink, as if thrusting a cross at a vampire. The effect on her parents was startling. They both screamed, "Please don't hurt us," before fleeing. Saesha's mother hurled herself into the toilet while her father ran out of the room. A stunned Saesha was left standing alone

A little later, they joined her for breakfast. Few words were spoken at the breakfast table that morning although suspicious glances were cast in Saesha's direction every now and then.

By the time Saesha had returned from school, her parents seemed to be their normal selves. She was desperate to find out what happened the night before but Reshmi had told her never to ask. That night there was a party at Aunty Rosie's house.

Waiting in the TV room, curiosity got the better of her and she decided to check on the adults. She crept down the corridor, following the raucous conversation and peals of laughter to their source. She poked her head around the corner and peered into the dining room to find a most remarkable sight. The aunties and uncles were acting like buffoons with bright glasses of Blink in their hands; her parents, however, were in a remote corner, looking on in horror at what was going on around them. Even more amazing was that Saesha's father was holding a glass of an amber beverage while her mother seemed to be sipping a red drink. They were not drinking Blink!

Saesha returned to the TV room, a beatific smile on her face. It had worked! Her parents weren't blinking any more. She happily sat down on the chair in front of the TV. But suddenly, an enormous shadow darkened the room. It belonged to Aunty Rosie still in a leopardskin suit with lumps of jiggling fat poking out everywhere. She wore a smirk and carried a glass of Blink as she leaned towards Saesha.

Still talking to yourself?"

"Sometimes, I guess," Saesha answered.

Aunty Rosie put her finger right up to Saesha's face and said, "Well, I can have you put in a place where they'll tie you to a chair, put spiders on your head, and give you worms to eat till you stop!"

Saesha's eyes went wide. "No, please don't!"

Aunty Rosie chortled.

"Rosie, what do you think you're doing?" said a voice behind her.

Saesha gasped. It was her father, with her mother. And they both looked really mad.

Aunty Rosie seemed unperturbed. "I was telling your daughter that she needs professional help."

Saesha's father glared at Aunty Rosie, his jaw clenched in rage. "My daughter is an angel. I would never change anything about her."

"Then, you're a fool," retorted Aunty Rosie

Now Saesha's mother moved forward. "I thought you had changed, Rosie. But it looks like the leopard, or at least the leopardskin, can't change its spots; however, perhaps I can change its colour." She grabbed the glass of Blink from Aunty Rosie's hand and poured it down her dress.

"My leopardskin dress! You've ruined it!" screeched Aunty Rosie.

"Actually, I think it's an improvement," Saesha's mother said, taking her daughter's hand.

Saesha's father turned to his wife and said, "Darling, let's go." He turned to the blubbering mess that was Aunty Rosie and said: "Thank you for this most unpleasant evening in this horrible house. We won't be returning," before walking out with his family.

During the drive home, Saesha listened with delight to her parents:

"I can't believe how boring those people are. All they do is drink Blink and act like fools," said Saesha's father.

"I know," replied her mother. "And the way that Asoka kept burping the whole evening – disgusting!"

"I agree," said her father. "We're never going to meet them again."

The next few months flew by. One night, she awoke to find a lone figure at her bedside. It was Reshmi.

"How wonderful to see you!" exclaimed Saesha.

Reshmi laughed. "You too, kid. I was passing by and just wanted to check how your family is doing."

"We're great!" declared Saesha. "My parents have stopped blinking. Our life has changed for the better – and it's all because of you. Thank you, Reshmi!"

Reshmi shook her head with a smile. "I didn't change your parents' minds. I simply provided them with an opportunity – they did the rest. It was their love for you that probably got them through."

"Well, I love them, too," said Saesha. "How's the Blink crisis?"

Reshmi breathed a sigh of relief. "It's over, finally. We've also negotiated a truce with the leprechauns so everything's going to be fine."

"How wonderful!" Then Saesha looked at Reshmi more closely. "Gosh, you're dressed so beautifully."

"I was wondering when you'd notice!" exclaimed Reshmi. "Look – a Chanel dress, Jimmy Choo shoes and a Birkin bag," she explained with a flourish.

"They sound expensive," said Saesha.

"Expensive for most – but not for the Tooth Fairy," Reshmi remarked, before giving Saesha a wink.

"You're the Tooth Fairy?" asked Saesha. "But what happened to the previous one?"

"Let's just say that she developed a little problem which required a visit from the Gambling Fairy. So she 'retired' and I got promoted to Tooth Fairy. Actually, that's why I'm here. Little Sarath Dias next door lost a baby tooth."

"Congratulations, Reshmi. I think you're great!" she said, hugging her.

Reshmi smiled. "You're not too bad yourself." Her wings fluttering, she floated above the bed. "Bye, Saesha."

"Wait!" shouted Saesha. "I've got one more question. When I prayed, I asked for help from everyone: Lord Buddha, Jesus, Vishnu, God of the Jews, God of Islam, Harry Potter and Barack Obama."

"I remember," said Reshmi. "So what do you want to know?"

"Which one of them sent you to me?"

"Well, let's just say that it wasn't Harry Potter," she declared before disappearing, her musical laugh continuing to echo in the room.

SUNRISE ON BUTTERFLY MOUNTAIN

Devika Brendon

"I remember when I was your age," Malathi's Grandmother said. "Every morning, I was so excited! Just because the sun rose up, and I could see it in the sky, and feel its warm rays getting hotter as the day turned towards noon."

"Soorya," said Malathi's little brother, who was practising his Sinhala letters in his writing book.

"Yes," their Grandmother said. "Soorya like on the box of matches, a red and gold and orange sun, lighting up the darkness all around it."

Malathi was in bed, being dosed with hot coriander tea, because she had been ill with a fever. Her little brother Ashvin had asked to be allowed to stay home from school too, so he could keep her company. Malathi felt weak, and her chest hurt from coughing.

Grandmother patted her hand sympathetically. Normally, this child was full of energy, jumping around, excited by just being alive. But the body sometimes needs to rest, and the old lady thought it was not too early for the children to learn this. Illness is a sign that the body needs to be still for a while.

"Let me tell you a story about sunrise," she said. "And I will use word pictures to describe it, and Ashvin can draw them for us, ok?"

Ashvin felt very important, and took out his set of coloured pencils.

"When I was a little bit older than you," Grandmother said, "my family climbed Sri Pada. Do you know what that is?"

"Adam's Peak!" said both kids.

"Yes, the sacred mountain of Sri Lanka," Grandmother said. "It is sacred to all religions. People climb it as a pilgrimage."

She explained that a pilgrimage was a long journey that a person went on, to test their strength and faith. They often make a vow or a promise and then go on the pilgrimage to show how determined they are to keep their promise.

"They start at the base of the mountain at night."

"After dinner?" Ashvin wanted to know.

"Yes, after a good but not too big dinner, because they have a long climb ahead. They carry food in their backpacks that is easy to eat while travelling."

" What food?" Malathi and Ashvin asked in unison.

"Like breakfast cereal, Lemon Puffs, chocolate bars, fruit, and Nippon Rolls," Grandmother said.

"At first, the path is just a dirt track, leading up to the base of the main ascent. Then there are steps that are carved into the side of the mountain. Steep steps, and a railing to hold onto. You climb and climb, up and up and up, through the darkness, all night."

The children's eyes were wide. How could you see the path ahead they wanted to know. If it was all dark.

"People carry torches and lamps," Grandmother said.

While the people climbed, she told them, they could hear wild animals around them, like sambhur deer barking, and the circular saw growl of a leopard, because the path was built through a wildlife park and jungle area.

"Kotiya," commented Ashvin, drawing spots on his picture.

Malathi closed her eyes for a moment. Sitting upright for so long, she was beginning to feel a little dizzy. Grandmother asked Ashvin to ask the cook for some tea and some fresh fruit juice and a plate of sliced mangos.

"I am okay," Malathi reassured them. She had been imagining the way the long procession of people would have looked, from a distance, climbing through the night, up the steep steps, with their fiery lanterns and electric torches, like a long, spiky ribbon of light, winding up the dark mountain.

Ashvin was drawing big spotted leopards, elephants, buffalo and deer all staring from the sides of the steps while the people climbed, with the lights from the flares and lanterns shining in their eyes. He drew dark glasses on some of them.

"On and on we climbed," said Grandmother, "until we were so tired that we had to stop and have some hot tea, like we are having now, and food. My legs felt heavy, and I did not know how far we had come or how far we still had to go before we reached the top.

"Yet, there were old people, and people on crutches, small children being carried on people's shoulders, all climbing – and everyone helped and encouraged each other. Each climbed alone, at their own pace, carrying their own burden, but all climbed in the same direction.

"After a while, I did not think about reaching the top or how long I had been climbing. I just kept going, following the steps of the people ahead of me, trying not to get in the way of those behind.

"Then slowly the sky started to lighten, and people put out their torches. We had reached the top, all of a sudden, and the sun was rising, like the red and gold and orange flaming star on the matchbox, and the long night and all its struggles and fears was over!

"We rang the bell at the top of the mountain, shared our breakfast cereal with others, just eating it by the handful from the box, without milk, and rested a little while we waited to see the twin shadow of the peak, growing long on the ground below.

"The sun was warming up as it rose, dissolving the early morning mists until they all faded away and the sky was clear. On the way down, we could see birds coming out to dry their wings so they could fly – and there were butterflies – so many butterflies, of every colour and size – some like bright jewels, some looking as if they were made of coloured tissue paper, all fluttering around us, drinking from the flowers and plants which were heavy with dew. Just like you two thirstily drink the fruit juice!" she said, and the children laughed.

"Why are the butterflies different colours?" asked Malathi. "Is it because of the different coloured flowers they eat?"

"Will I turn orange like the mango?" asked Ashvin, anxious because he had eaten most of it. Malathi was still not able to have much solid food.

Grandmother explained that Sri Pada, also called Adam's Peak, has another name as well: Butterfly Mountain. She said, "Whenever I feel old or tired, or have been not well, like Malathi has been these past days, I remember the butterflies dancing, their colours glittering around me as I came back down the mountain path, down to the last step, along the dirt track, and back to the guesthouse where we were staying. After illness, we become well and healthy again; after night there is daybreak; and when the sun rises we should rise with it."

"Him," said Ashvin, solemnly. "We rise with him. Soorya. The sun."

Ashvin gave his Grandmother the picture he had drawn and ran to get some more fruit.

"You have to go to school tomorrow," said Malathi, calling after him. She already seemed better.

the end

Afdhel Aziz grew up in Sri Lanka, and now lives in New York. His favorite children's book writers growing up were Enid Blyton, Dr Seuss, Shel Silverstein, and C.S. Lewis.

 Nanda Pethiyagoda Wanasundera is a journalist who has been a teacher and the head librarian of the Overseas School of Colombo. She has written eight books, one of which is a collection of folk tales of Sri Lanka.

 Alexa Harris is a German/American researcher who has worked for development organizations. She currently lives in Sri Lanka with her husband and their three-year-old daughter, who she hopes, will enjoy this story when older.

 Sanjaya Senanayake is a doctor who loves to write stories that make children smile.

 Ameena Hussein is a writer and publisher. She believes that Sri Lankan children should have the chance to read stories about themselves.

 Pia Fernando-Sonderegger was born in Switzerland, and has lived in the USA, Italy, Spain and since 1999 in Sri Lanka. She has published short stories and prose in Switzerland, Germany and Sri Lanka.

Asgar Hussein is a journalist, poet and fiction writer. His works include *Termite Castle* (which won the State Literary Award) and *The Mirror of Paradise* (shortlisted for the Gratiaen Prize). This is his first story for children.

Devika Brendon is a reader & writer of stories, who teaches English Literature to students, hoping to show them how exciting words can be.

Mary Anne Mohanraj was born in Colombo. She lives near Chicago with her partner, Kevin, their children, Kavya and Anand, and dog, Ellie. She has written several books for adults, and a children's book, *The Poet's Journey*.

Ameena Hussein is an author and co-founder of the Perera Hussein Publishing House. The first collection of *MilkRice*, edited by her, received rave reviews and was taught in Sri Lankan schools. She has just released the second collection of *MilkRice 2*.

Created in 2005, POPSICLE BOOKS is the children's arm of the Perera-Hussein Publishing House. Its mission is to create interesting and original books which children will love, giving them a sense of place while opening windows of learning, diversity and culture.

Mythil's Secret

Paduma meets the Sunbird

Butterflies Kisses and Turtle Tears

Mona's Mission Impossible

Asiri's Quest

MilkRice

MilkRice 2

Angel Games and Little Flames

Three friends and the Big Wave

The Runaway Christmas Tree